T0368516

AuthorHouse™
1663 Liberty Drive
Bloomington, IN 47403
www.authorhouse.com
Phone: 833-262-8899

This book is printed on acid-free paper.

ISBN: 979-8-8230-3619-1 (sc)
ISBN: 979-8-8230-3620-7 (hc)
ISBN: 979-8-8230-3618-4 (e)

Library of Congress Control Number: 2024922151

Print information available on the last page.

Published by AuthorHouse 11/20/2024

authorHOUSE®

Dr. O'Hara: Ah Africa, giraffe, zebra, lions, antelope, termite mounds, acacia, and baobab trees! I can't believe there are still some left, in this day, and age.

Dr. Mugadi: Sean, welcome to Kenya.
Tsavo National Park
Dr. O'Hara: Meru, so good to see you.
Dr. Mugadi: We will have a long drive to the reserve and lots to talk about.

Dr. Mugadi: There are so many examples of human versus animal, with the animal losing every time. I'm just saying that nature has always had a balance until we came along. We have changed the earth more in the last 100 years, than nature has, in the last million years. We keep living for today and not for tomorrow. See the goats drinking at the waterhole. The herders have guns to shoot any cheetahs on site. The open savannah is shrinking and this drives animals into encroaching farms looking for food.

Dr. Mugadi: Thank you very much for coming around the world to help a friend.

Dr. O'Hara: Glad to help. What happens 10,000 miles away will eventually affect us all.

Dr. Mugadi: Let me explain one of our biggest problems. Sorry we have quite a drive to the reserve.

Dr. O'Hara: That's OK, this is my first trip to Africa and I'm enjoying every minute of it.

Dr. Mugadi: How is everything at your zoo, in Oregon?

Dr. O'Hara: Good, thank you. Every year we move forward in helping to promote conservation and reproduce more rare animals.

Dr. Mugadi: Sean, I ask you. What good is it to breed more rare animals when you can't put them back? Our biggest problem are habitat loss, pollution, overpopulation, and disrupting migration patterns. We may be entering another mass extinction era?

Dr. Mugadi: Let me now explain why I called for help. It's the bongo. The Tsavo National Park has about 200 bongo left. With their federal protection, we went from 35, five years ago to the current 200. Every year they cross the Nakuru River and migrate 150 kilometers north to the Gemsbok National Park, for greener pastures during the dry season. At Gemsbok, they have better pastures, allowing them to eat more, gain healthier weights, breed, give birth, and relax. Then at the beginning of the Gemsbok dry season, they migrate back to Tsavo for the same reason. They have probably done this for thousands of years. Here's the problem. A new dam will be completed before their migration starts over the next few days, blocking their migration route. Once the dam is filled, they will not be able to cross the Nakuru River. The new dam will make the river 50 times wider and below the dam, the river will be too swift to cross, drowning those who attempt to cross. I've tried to explain the situation to the government, but they have other priorities.

Dr. Mugadi: We do not know exactly what will happen, other than this rare African hoofstock may likely die out. Here is their current dilemma. If they travel further south along the river, they will run into the big city of Arusha and be killed in the busy highways. If they travel north along the river, they will enter farms and unprotected areas, where poachers are plentiful. If they return to Tsavo, the grass and plants will soon dry up and they will starve. They cannot travel east of Tsavo due to the Mahali Mountains. The only hope is for them to travel northeast to The Okapi National Park, but instinct has them travelling to Gemsbok to the northwest. Perhaps they are trapped and will become extinct?

Dr. Mugadi: Exactly, complete with new shopping malls.
Dr. Mugadi: If the bongo would only use a bridge or tunnel to cross the new dam?
Dr. Mugadi: We tried, remember their instinct to migrate is a thousand-year-old habit.
Welcome to
Tsavo National Park
Kenya
Dr. O'Hara: Let me guess, the new dam will be supplying electricity and water to the growing human towns and suburbs?
Dr. O'Hara: Can you feed them during the dry season and keep them in Tsavo?

Dr. Mugadi: Finally, we are home.
Dr. Mugadi: That reminds me. Please do not go out alone at night, without an escort, for there are occasional leopards, lions, even hippo.
Dr. Mugadi: Let us go indoors to meet my family, have dinner, and relax from your trip.
Tsavo National Park
Dr. O'Hara: Look at all the free-roaming animals.
Dr. O'Hara: I think I'll stay inside.

Dr. O'Hara: Sidi, nice to meet you and Mali. What a beautiful home and stunning artwork.
Dr. Mugadi: Sidi, this is Sean O'Hara
Dr. Mugadi: And this is my son, Mali.
Sidi: Nice to meet you Sean. Welcome to our home. I have heard nice things about you.
Sidi: Please sit while I serve dinner.

Dr. O'Hara: I love to taste new foods. This is delicious.
Dr. O'Hara: I brought a gift from Oregon, for all of you.
Dr. Mugadi: Before retiring, I'll show you a map of the reserve and where we will be working on the bongo herd tomorrow.
Sidi: It is Meru's favourite, barbequed pork, wild yams, and spinach.
Mali: Thank you Sean.

Dr. Mugadi: Here is a wall map of the local area. Here are the three National Parks, City of Arusha, Nakuru and Okavango Rivers, farmland, and The Mahale Mountains. The end of this stick is where the bongo herd is.

Dr. Mugadi: It's getting late. I'll show you your room. In the morning, we will check the bongo herd, which is headed toward the new dam.

Dr. O'Hara: Now I can really visualize the problem. Hmmm, lots of obstacles, very complex, troubles ahead.

Dr. O'Hara: Sounds good. It's been a long day. Meru, if some how, we could only break the bongo's thousand-year habit of travelling north, and instead travel east to Okapi National Park. Hmmm. Getting sleepy, time for bed.

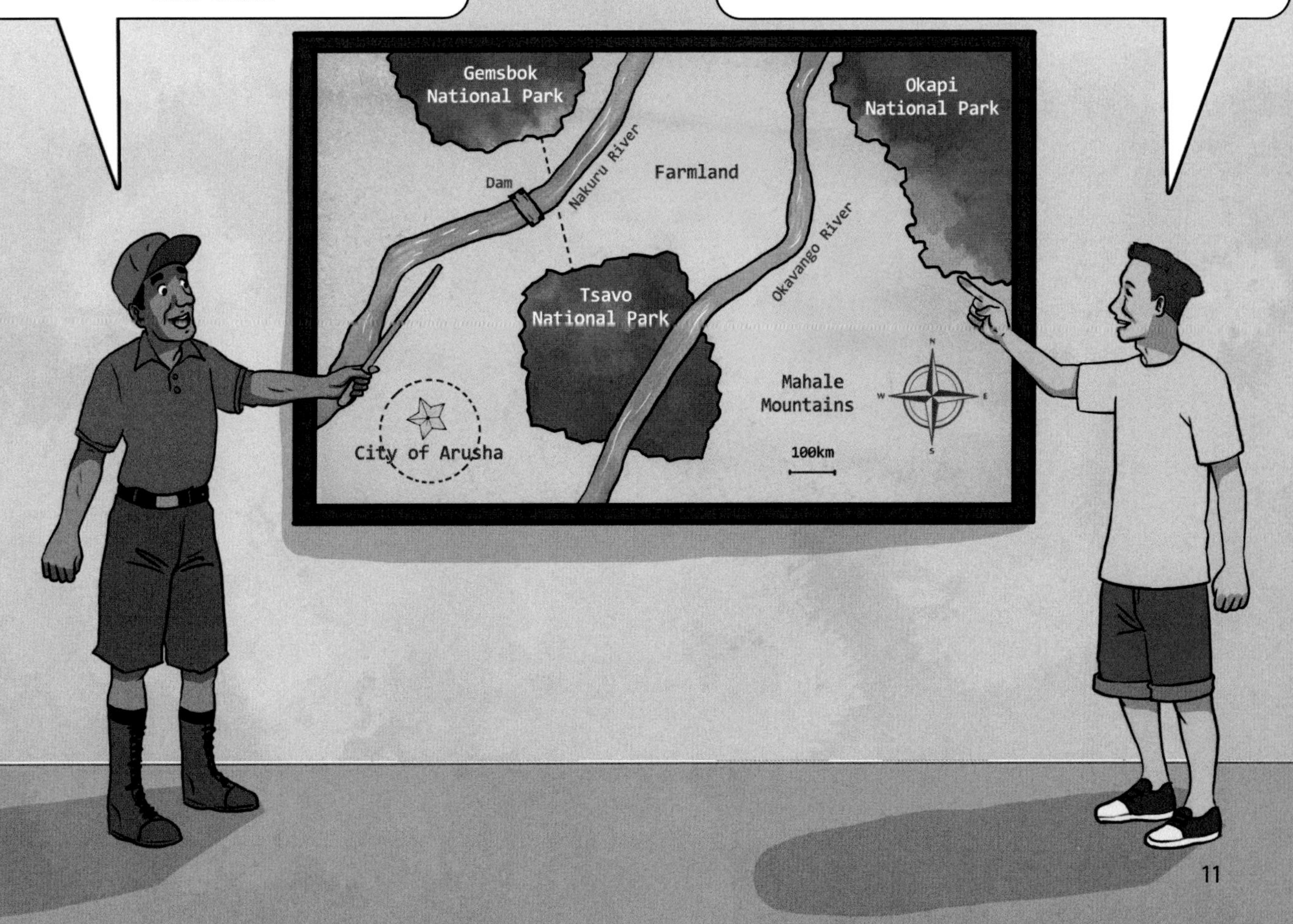

To Gemsbok
To Okapi
Turn Right
Ahead
Follow the leader.
Follow the leader.
Follow the leader.

Dr. Mugadi: What's going on? What's all the commotion about? Maybe I thought a lion jumped through the window.
Dr. Mugadi: It's 3am in the morning! Sean you must have a serious case of jet lag.
Dr. Mugadi: OK, but first to the kitchen for a midnight snack while I listen to your kooky dream.
Dr. O'Hara: I got it! I got it! Yes!
Dr. O'Hara: Meru, I know it will work. My dream will work.
Dr. O'Hara: I think I have a solution to the bongo problem. Quick to the wall map and I will explain.

Dr. O'Hara: Let's go over this again. It's safe passage for bongo to go from Tsavo National Park to Okapi National Park, correct?
Dr. Mugadi: Correct.
Dr. O'Hara: The timing and direction of migration starts with the herd dominant male?
Dr. Mugadi: Correct.
Dr. O'Hara: With today's robotics you can build a life-size bongo robot, where even the rest of the bongo herd will be fooled.
Dr. Mugadi: Wait. Let me guess. We make a robot, as the dominant male, who will lead the herd to Okapi National Park, establishing a new migration pattern?
Dr. O'Hara: Exactly!
Dr. Mugadi: That's a crazy dream. Silly dream. Insane dream. You know, your dream may just work?
Gemsbok National Park
Okapi National Park
Dam
Nakuru River
Farmland
Okavango River
Tsavo National Park
Mahale Mountains
City of Arusha
100km
N
W
E
S

Dr. Mugadi: No problem, we will tranquilize the dominant males and transport them to Okapi. Then the herd will only have our robot bongo to follow.
Dr. Mugadi: Question. Who will build this fancy robot and with little time to spare?
Dr. Mugadi: Sean, that's a big 10-4! We are ready to start the "Save the Bongo Project"
Dr. O'Hara: One problem I forsee is what about the real dominant bongo males?
Dr. O'Hara: No worries. My brother Craig works at JPL. You know, Jet Propulsion Laboratory. It's managed by Cal Tech and funded by NASA. They are #1 in robotic spacecraft.
Dr. O'Hara: Besides being my younger brother, he owes me.
Sidi: What are you "Peter Pans" jumping up at 3am for?
Dr. Mugadi: Save the bongo
Dr. O'Hara: I like that, "Operation Save the Bongo".
Gemsbok National Park
Okapi National Park
Dam
Nakuru River
Farmland
River
Tsavo National Park
Mahale Mountains
City of Arusha
100km

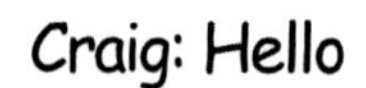
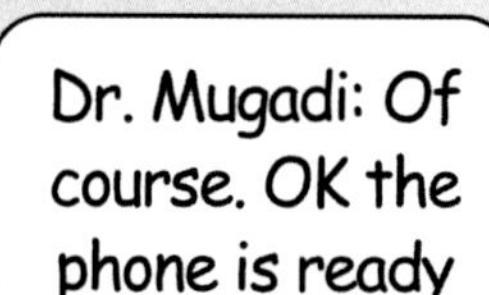

Dr. O'Hara: Quick. Can I use your satellite phone?
Dr. Mugadi: Of course. OK the phone is ready
Dr. O'Hara: Hello, Craig. Calling Craig.
CALIFORNIA
KENYA
Craig: Hello
Dr. O'Hara: Craig, it's your brother sean
Craig: Hey Sean. Mom told me you were in Africa
Dr. O'Hara: Yes, I'm here. Listen we have a big problem. We need you to develop a life-size robotic bongo with AI.
Craig: Bongo is that a drum?
Dr. Mugadi: No, it's the African antelope.
Craig: Well, give me the details.
Dr. O'Hara: It's gotta look, act, smell like a bongo, travel 200km, cross rivers, dodge lions and poachers.
Craig: Wait, I'm still trying to write bongo down.

CALIFORNIA
KENYA
Dr. O'Hara: Craig, this is my good friend, Meru.
Craig: Nice to meet you Meru.
Dr. Mugadi: Nice to meet you Craig.
Dr. Mugadi: Craig, this robot will face several dangerous obstacles and will need some "secret weapons".
Craig: I know what a gazelle looks like. Can I make a gazelle?
Dr. O'Hara: No!
Dr. O'Hara: We can't explain everything right now, but I will send you bongo specifications.
Craig: The students at JPL do need a robot project to do and this would be perfect.
Dr O'Hara: Oh and Craig, one more thing. We need this bongo robot in 1 week, please.
Craig: What! One week!
Craig: Why couldn't you open a vet practice down the street here? OK, I better get going on the project. Hey isn't 3am over there? This is Craig signing out. Good-bye.

Dr. Mugadi: Did you have plenty of breakfast?

Dr. O'Hara: Yes. Sidi is the best cook. Does she have a sister?

Dr. Mugadi: Sorry Sean, she only has brothers. Well, the boys are almost ready. We have a scout team locating the bongo herd. We will travel together in the Pegasus.

Dr. O'Hara: I love the new Pegasus SUV.

Dr. Mugadi: Have you seen all the features in the Pegasus?

Dr. O'Hara: Not yet. Can you show me?

Dr. Mugadi: As they say in America, "let's go check it out".

Dr. Mugadi: Let's see. It has 100% composite body making it light, yet strong.
Dr. Mugadi: No it's completely electric, from solar and/or charging. Fossil fuels are out, "old man".
Dr. Mugadi: The whole body is a solar cell. The "green house" paint traps the sunlight photons, which bounce back and forth increasing the battery charging.
Dr. O'Hara: Is it a hybrid?
Dr. O'Hara: Where are the solar cells?
Tsavo National Park

Dr. Mugadi: The windshield is an all weather, heads-up display with voice command. It comes with a 360 degree complete, wrap-around airbag system for safety. These new cars also "talk to each other" on the road and avoid car collisions.
Dr. Mugadi: Watch what happens when I push this button.
Dr. Mugadi: You get pop up knobbes on your tires for off-road conditions. Push the button again and the knobbes pop down.

REAR VIEW CAMERA

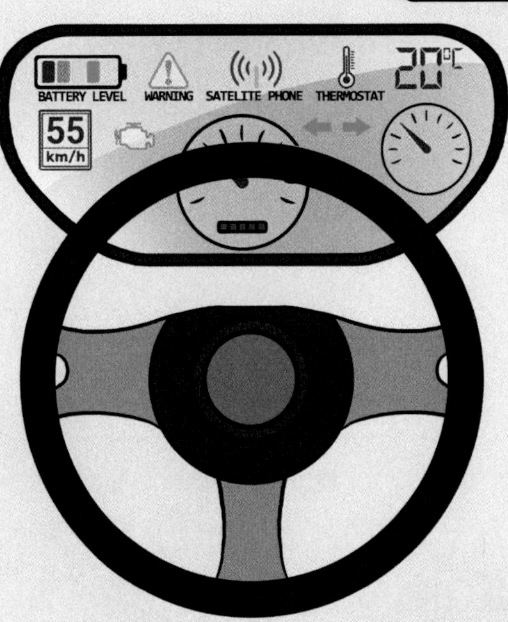
BATTERY LEVEL
WARNING
SATELITE PHONE
THERMOSTAT
20°C
55
km/h

Dr. O'Hara: Very impressive, but these tires won't get you out of a mudhole.
Dr. O'Hara: Whooo!

Puuyoop!!

Dr. O'Hara: So where is the 400-pound battery hiding?
Dr. Mugadi: You won't find it because the car frame is also the battery.

Dr. O'Hara: What does this button do that says "trailer"?

Dr. O'Hara: That's it, you sold me one.

Dr. Mugadi: You'll love this. When you need a trailer to haul stuff, just push that button and the back end extends out producing a trailer. Watch.

Helicopter Pilot: Air-One to Dr. Mugadi. Air-One to Dr. Mugadi.
Tsavo National Park

Dr. Mugadi: That's the helicopter! Go ahead Air-One.

Dr. Mugadi: Roger. On our way.

Dr. Mugadi: We also have a few bongo fitted with satellite collars that tell us their locations.

Dr. Mugadi: Dr. Mugadi to headquarters.

Dr. Mugadi: We are leaving now. Please inform Dr. Ruvubi and Okapi Headquarters of our plan. Code sign is "Operation Save The Bongo".

Tsavo National Park
Tsavo National Park
Tsavo National Park

Dr. Mugadi: Dr. Mugadi to Air- One.
Helicopter Pilot: This is Air- One. Go ahead.
Dr. Mugadi: We are about 1km south of herd. We will go ahead of the herd to intercept the dominant males.
Helicopter Pilot: Roger. We will continue to patrol the park for poachers. Call Air Cargo when ready to transport bongo.
Dr. Mugadi: Copy that Air-One. Thank you.
REAR VIEW CAMERA
BATTERY LEVEL
WARNING
SATELITE PHONE
THERMOSTAT
20°C
60
km/h

Dr. Mugadi: There they are. These are the dominant males leading the pack.

Dr. O'Hara: What a beautiful site. I've only seen them in zoos. Seeing them in the wild in their natural habitat is amazing.

Dr. Mugadi: Sean. I think I have a plan. This valley goes another 10kms and I bet we can use the rocket nets and catch the dominant males.

Dr. O'Hara: Sounds like a plan to me.

Dr. Mugadi: Dr. Mugadi to Chobe.

Chobe: This is Chobe. Go ahead boss.

Dr. Mugadi: We spotted the bongo down the Carroo Valley. They are headed your way. Please set up the rocket nets to capture about 10 bongo.

Chobe: 10-4 boss.

Chobe: Chobe to Dr. Mugadi.
Dr. Mugadi: Go ahead Chobe.
Chobe: The nets are almost ready. We baited the target area with alfalfa, sweet feed, and fruit. Over
Dr. Mugadi: Good job Chobe. We will meet up with you soon. The bongo should be there in about 1 hour.
Gumpti: Hey this fruit is pretty good.
Chobe: Roger that. Hey Gumpti, the fruit is supposed to be for the bongo.

KAPOOW!
KAPOOW!
Chobe: Say when boss.
KAPOOW!
KAPOOW!
Dr. Mugadi: Chobe are you ready? Here they come.
Dr. Mugadi: Steady. Steady. They are stopping for the food.
KAPOOW!
Dr. Mugadi: Now Chobe. Now. Fire.

Chobe: One got away boss.
Dr. Mugadi: Good show Chobe!
Dr. Mugadi: No worries. We will catch him later. You still get an A for today.

Dr. Mugadi: Sean, I will give each bongo a tranquilizer to reduce stress and injury. Why don't you take care of physical exams, blood sample collection, microchip, and skin biopsy for DNA analysis.
Dr. Mugadi: Next, I will give injections for capture stress. Chobe should be setting up the portable chute system for loading into crates.
Dr. O'Hara: 10-4.

Chobe: Chobe to Dr. Mugadi.
Chobe: The last truck is being loaded
Dr. Mugadi: This is Dr. Mugadi.
Dr. Mugadi: Right. Call the Chinook for pick-up. There is a good landing zone, a few kms east of you.
Tsavo National Park

KENYA AIR FORCE
Chinook Pilot: Chinook One to Chobe.
Chobe: Go ahead this is Chobe.
Chinook Pilot: I see your smoke marker. Stand clear, we are landing.
Chobe: Roger.

KENYA AIR FORCE
Tsavo National Park
Dr. Mugadi: Hi Dr. Ruvubi.
Dr. Ruvubi: Hello Meru. This must be Dr. O'Hara, from Oregon? Hope the bugs here don't eat you alive.
Dr. O'Hara: Nice to meet you. I heard you are the wildlife vet at Okapi National Park.
Dr. Ruvubi: Sidi filled me in on this kooky plan of a robot somehow changing the migration plan to Okapi instead of Gemsbok? How many males did you net?
Dr. Mugadi: We got nine, one got away.
Dr. Ruvubi: So, is the robot secret weapon here yet?
Dr. O'Hara: My brother and his team are still making it.
Dr. Ruvubi: Heh. The rest of the herd will be here soon. We may be just wasting our time with this kooky plan?
Dr. Mugadi: Doc, all we can do is our best. Besides, we are out of options.
Dr. O'Hara: 10-4.
Dr. Mugadi: Sean, Dr. Ruvubi is very opinionated.

Gumti: Anybody got their ears on?
Dr. Mugadi: Go ahead Gumti.
Gumti: Located the bongo that got away.
Dr. Mugadi: Good, where are you?
Gumti: Seven kilometers north of the netting. GPS #0.765 over.
Dr. Mugadi: On our way. It's getting late so we'll dart in the morning. You men take turns watching it over the night and we'll call at sun-up.
Gumti: Roger.

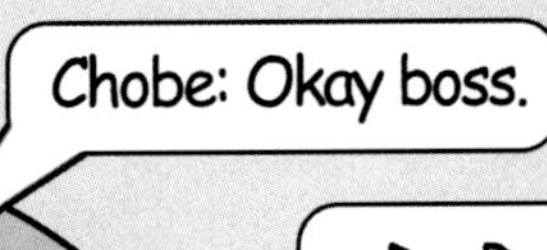
Dr. Ruvubi: Okay Meru. We've loaded up the Chinook with the bongo and ready to go. We'll keep them in a corral at Okapi until you're ready.
Dr. Mugadi: Thanks Dr. Ruvubi. Let's go Sean.
Dr. Mugadi: Chobe, we'll meet you back at base camp tomorrow.
Chobe: Okay boss.

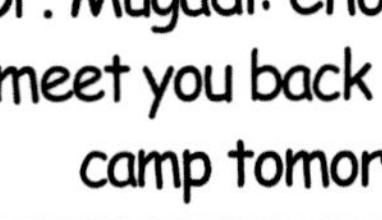

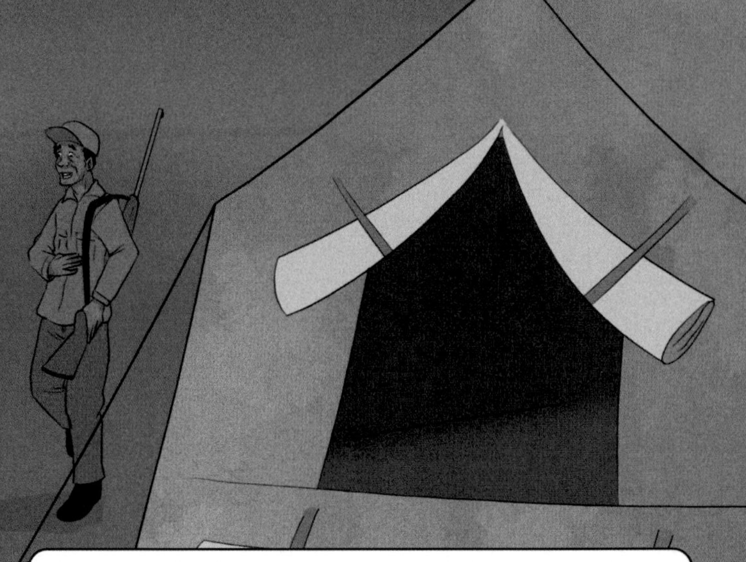

Dr. O'Hara: Back home we say, I'm so hungry I could eat a horse. You guys in Africa have bigger animals and bigger appetites.
Dr. Mugadi: I'm so hungry I could eat an elephant.
Dr. O'Hara: I see that saving animal species is not a big priority here either. I mean you would think the whole world would be concerned and help these bongo. Every animal on Earth is connected to 10 other and if one becomes extinct, then that affects the other 10.
Dr. Mugadi: Don't forget the plants. They are connected too.
Dr. O'Hara: You know Meru, it's like planet Earth is a big aquarium, with all these plants and animals that are connected and depended on each other.
Dr. Mugadi: That's the problem Sean, we forget that we are one of these animals living in this big aquarium.
Dr. O'Hara: I'll call Craig tomorrow to see how they're doing with the robot.
Dr. Mugadi: Good. Oh by the way, during the night if the watch guard yells Hatari, then grab your gun and every man for himself. Hatari is Swahili for danger. Generally used for lions, hippo, elephants, etc.

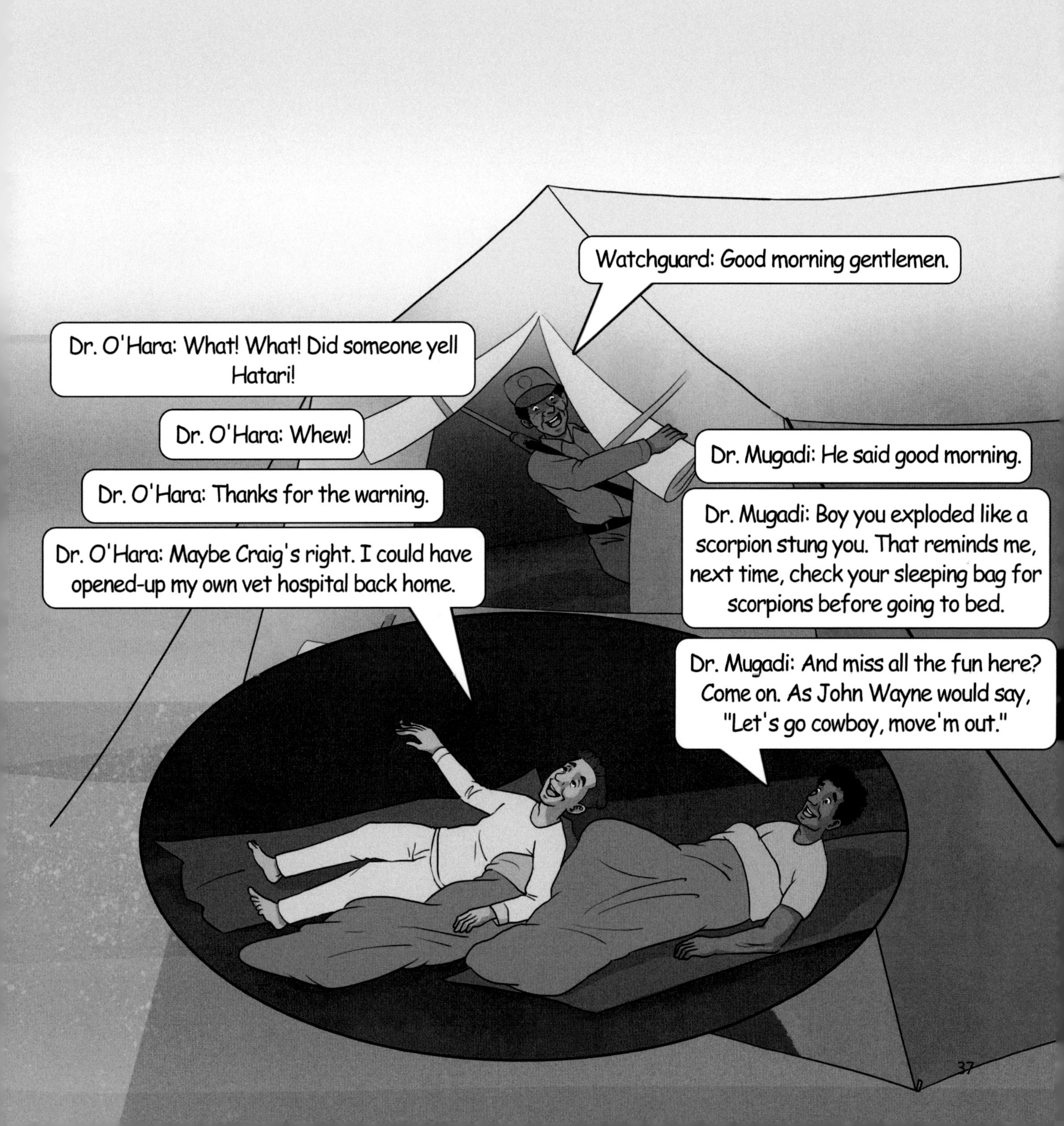
Watchguard: Good morning gentlemen.
Dr. O'Hara: What! What! Did someone yell Hatari!
Dr. O'Hara: Whew!
Dr. Mugadi: He said good morning.
Dr. O'Hara: Thanks for the warning.
Dr. Mugadi: Boy you exploded like a scorpion stung you. That reminds me, next time, check your sleeping bag for scorpions before going to bed.
Dr. O'Hara: Maybe Craig's right. I could have opened-up my own vet hospital back home.
Dr. Mugadi: And miss all the fun here? Come on. As John Wayne would say, "Let's go cowboy, move'm out."

Chobe: Chobe to Dr. Mugadi.
Dr. Mugadi: Go ahead Chobe.
Chobe: The dominant male bongo just got up and is slowly walking north. GPS #0.770 over.
Dr. Mugadi: Copy. ETA about 30 minutes.
Chobe: Roger.
Dr. Mugadi: As they say in America, "it's showtime".
Dr. O'Hara: You watch too much TV.

Chobe: Dr. Mugadi over here. Quiet please.

Chobe: Over there, down this hill. See him?

Dr. O'Hara: Yes, and it's set for 400 kilos body weight.

Dr. Mugadi: Where is he?

Dr. Mugadi: OK Sean, you have the dart rifle. Is the anesthesia set on hoofstock?

Dr. Mugadi: Fire when ready.

Dr. Mugadi: Good shot!

Dr. Mugadi: Sean, is the dart sensor connected to your communicator?
Dr. Mugadi: He ran off into the forest. Which way?
Dr. O'Hara: Yes, and everything looks good. Heart rate is 40 beats per minute, respiratory rate is 12 breathes per minute, organ functions are normal.
Dr. O'Hara: He's 105 meters northeast. Approach with caution since he is currently in heavy sedation status.

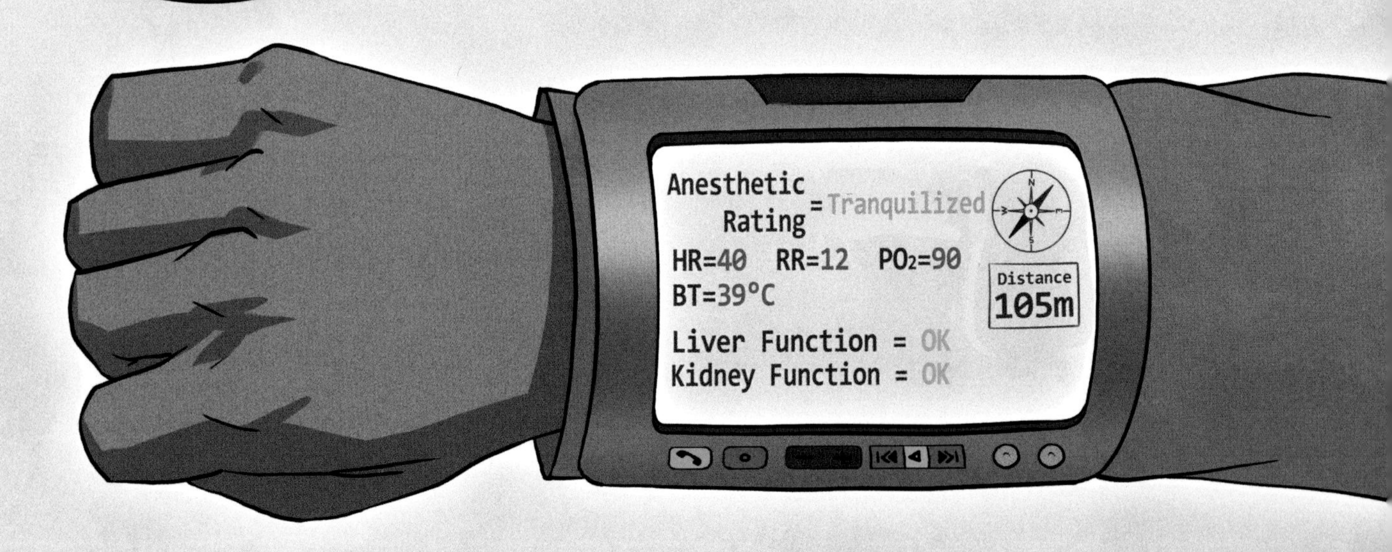
Anesthetic Rating = Tranquilized
HR=40 RR=12 PO2=90
BT=39°C
Liver Function = OK
Kidney Function = OK
Distance
105m

Dr. Mugadi: His physical exam is fine. He's had his meds and microchip so we'll load him up after you finish taking samples.
Chobe: Dr. Mugadi, a herd of elephants is headed this way.
Dr. Mugadi: Stand guard! Sean, just keep doing your job. Hopefully with all the commotion here, the elephants should go around us.

Chobe: Everyone stand clear.
Dr. O'Hara: 10-4
Dr. Mugadi: Okay Chobe, use the truck winch to pull him into the crate.
Dr. Mugadi: As soon as he's in the crate Sean, you can give him the reversal injection and wake him up.

Dr. O'Hara: Meru, it's kind of muddy around here. Can your truck get us out of here with crate and bongo?
Dr. O'Hara: Actually I'm anxious to push that button this time.
Dr. O'Hara: Sweet!
Tsavo National Park
Dr. Mugadi: Easy Chobe.
Dr. Mugadi: It's time to use the pop-up knobbes.
Dr. Mugadi: Sean, you can not only push the pop-up knobbe button, but drive back too.

Tsavo National Park

Craig: Hello brother. We are almost done. Still need a couple of days. When does the migration start?
Craig: Your zoo hoofstock keepers have been very helpful on the design, anticipated problems, even how bongo act. We shaved some hair from a real bongo. It even smells like a bongo.
Craig: The added secret weapon is what's taking so long. The students gets an A+ grade on this robot. We will be able to control it from our control center here in Pasadena.
Craig: Oh, his name. Yes, his name is "Bingo" the bongo.

BATTERY LEVEL
WARNING
SATELITE PHONE
THERMOSTAT
20
Dr. O'Hara: Hello Craig.
Dr. O'Hara: In a couple of days.
Dr. O'Hara: Good because if the real bongo suspect something "fishy" they will run from it. Does your prototype have a name?
Dr. O'Hara: Plus, we need about 10 hours to fly it here.

Craig: OK I'm going to get back to work. We're like busy bees here.
MOTOR
Dr. O'Hara: Good job. Let me know when you are done. If you can fly it to Casa Blanca, Morocco, then the Kenyan air force will pick it up there.
Dr. O'Hara: Talk to you later.

Chobe: Chobe to Dr. Mugadi, Chobe to Dr. Mugadi.
Dr. Mugadi: Go ahead Chobe, this is Dr. Mugadi.
Chobe: The bongo herd are starting to wander out of the park, over.
Dr. Mugadi: Don't know Sean. Don't know. Pause... We can't dart 200 bongo. They would scatter. Can't net them, we would need a net 5 kilometers wide. All we can do at this point is hope our plan works.
Chobe: 10-4 Boss.
Dr. Mugadi: 10-4 Sean. Chobe Stay with the herd as best as you can. We will meet you there tomorrow.
Tsavo National Park
Dr. O'Hara: Is it too late?
Dr. O'Hara: Don't be so hard on yourself Meru. Let's take Mali to the river and catch some fish for dinner before it gets dark.

CALIFORNIA
KENYA
Craig: Hello Sean.
Dr. O'Hara: Hi Craig. Tell us good news.
Craig: Bingo the bongo flew out this morning and should be in Morocco about now. I assume it would be dropped from the air.
Dr. O'Hara: Good idea, that would save time. You see yesterday the bongo herd left the park. Wait, what? You
Craig: Don't worry, we have a parachute in it. We also have it programmed to travel to Okapi National Park. Wait until you see it. The eyes are cameras that will send us real time images.
Dr. O'Hara: Wow!
Dr. Mugadi: Let me contact the Kenyan Air Force for a drop in the morning.
Dr. Mugadi: Awesome. Craig, thank you and your students.
Craig: You're welcome. Let me know when it's parachuted and I will turn it on. The battery for Bingo will only last for about a week.
Dr. O'Hara: Thanks again. Call you later.
Dr. O'Hara: Did I tell you Meru, Craig is my favourite brother.
Craig: Hey Sean, I heard that. I'm his only brother Dr. Meru.

Dr. Mugadi: It's hard enough to monitor them in the park. Well, now they only have two directions to survive, either back to Tsavo or towards Okapi.

Dr. Mugadi: Should be here soon Chobe.

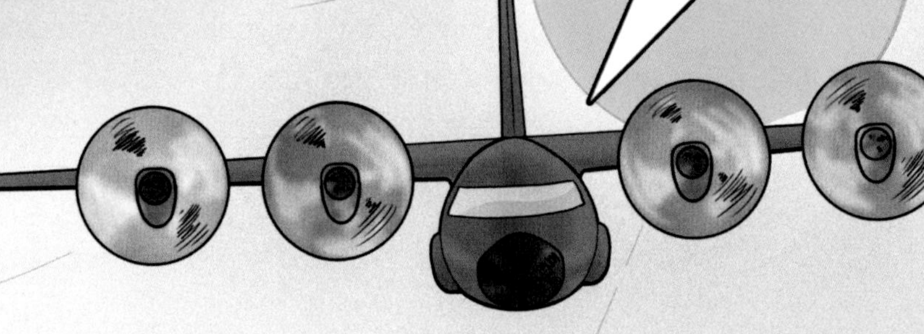
Hercules Plane: Cargo-1 to Tsavo. Cargo-1 to Tsavo.
Hercules Plane: This is Captain Tshivanga, we have your Bingo the bongo. Where do you want it dropped, over.
Hercules Plane: Roger. ETA 5 minutes.

Dr. Mugadi: This is Dr. Mugadi for Tsavo. Go ahead.
Dr. Mugadi: Captain we are just west of the park, GPS #779. If you could just drop it 3 kilometeers east of us at 0.776 over.
Dr. Mugadi: Roger we will look for you over and out.

Dr. O'Hara: Like you said Meru. It's showtime.

Hercules Plane: Cargo-1 to Dr. Mugadi.
Hercules Plane: Dropping your package in T-minus two minutes, over.
Hercules Plane: This is Captain Tshivanga. Here's your package Tsavo. Glad to help and good luck.
Hercules Plane: Roger that.
Dr. Mugadi: Go ahead.
Dr. Mugadi: Roger. We have a visual of your plane. We are ready.
Dr. Mugadi: Roger. Many thanks Captain. Have a safe flight back.
Chobe: I hear the buzz of the Hercules. Oh there it is.

Craig: Hello! Sean. Is it almost there yet?
Craig: Well, it passed its first test, the opening of the parachute. That's a good thing.
Craig: OK, we will send Bingo's camera images to your communicator.

Dr. O'Hara: Let me call Craig.
Dr. O'Hara: It's parachuting down. Quick turn it on.
Dr. O'Hara: Craig, the herd is just east of where Bingo is landing.
Dr. Mugadi: There it is! I see the parachute.

Dr. O'Hara: Hey Craig. I think something is wrong. My communicator only shows green throughout the screen.
Craig: That's a parachute brother. We are just going through a quick safety check on all the operating systems.

Craig: Bingo the bongo is ready to go to work guys!
Dr. O'Hara: Does Bingo know where east is?
Craig: Relax Sean. It has the equivalent of that compass ball that Aunt Julia always had on the dashboard of her car. Remember that?
Dr. O'Hara: OK I trust you. Yes, I remember the compass ball.

N
W
E
S
Craig: Here is test #2 coming up. If they accept Bingo, as one of their own.
Dr. Mugadi: Up ahead and to the right. There is one of the bongo from the herd.
Craig: How's the picture on your communicator?
Dr. O'Hara: Nice and clear.

Dr. Mugadi: Craig, just walk around and mingle with the herd. If any males challenge you, do not back down. You have to establish yourself as the leader.

Craig: I think we are getting the hang of it.

Craig: What if challenged?

Dr. Mugadi: Most are bluffs. If a bongo stands its ground, then just charge and if you have to, butt heads. Keeping in mind that an injury may lead to wounds, infection, or an injury not allowing them to finish the migration.

Dr. Mugadi: Craig, can Bingo take some punches?

Dr. Mugadi: It will be kind of monotonous, but we must do this until the herd accepts Bingo, as the dominant male. You can shut him down at night to converse energy.

Craig: Bingo is made of titanium, composites, and strong glue. In other words, yes, he's pretty tough. Hey passed test #2, the herd has accepted Bingo, as a real bongo.

Craig: Hear that guys!

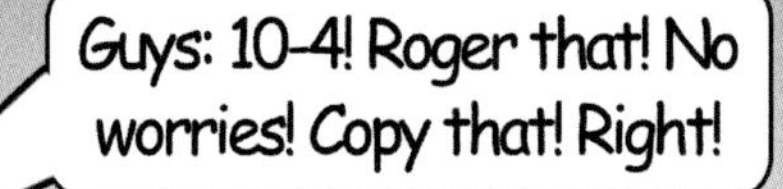

Guys: 10-4! Roger that! No worries! Copy that! Right!

Dr. O'Hara: I think the herd may be ready Craig. Start migrating toward Okapi. We will follow about 5 kilometers behind.
Dr. O'Hara: It's starting to work! That young bongo is walking toward Bingo. The others are just looking though.
Dr. Mugadi: Give it a moment Sean.
Dr. O'Hara: There they go! It's working!
Dr. Mugadi: Looks like they are all staring at Bingo. All we need is one to follow and the rest will do the same. Once they start migrating, we will follow in the Pegasus.
Craig: Well guys, we passed test #3. The migration.

Craig: Dr. Mugadi, how many days to Okapi?
Craig: Dr. Mugadi, one of my students just spotted a lion up ahead. I will focus on her. She is crouched on that hill peeking through the bushes. See her.
Craig: OK, but one lion won't challenge the whole herd, will it?
Dr. Mugadi: About 2 days.
Dr. Mugadi: Craig. Stop Bingo now!
Dr. Mugadi: That lion is the chaser. She will chase the herd toward an awaiting pride. Turn the camera 360. There must be a bunch of lions waiting for them. The lion coat color blends in well with the dry grass, making them almost invisible.

Craig: I see them to the north. Wow, there's about 15 lions waiting to attack.
Dr. Mugadi: There, stop Craig.
Dr. O'Hara: Craig, the herd may scatter every which way. If the lions attack. This may confuse the new migration direction.
BATTERY LEVEL
WARNING
SATELITE PHONE
THERMOSTAT
15 km/h

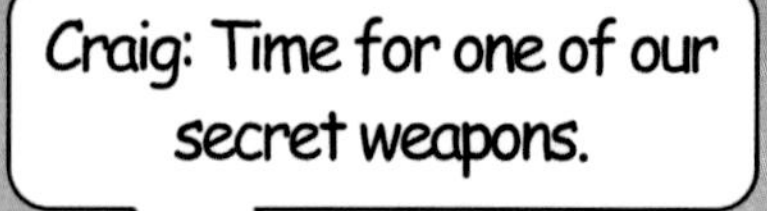

Craig: Time for one of our secret weapons.

Dr. O'Hara: What is it?

Craig: Catnip! Your zoo was able to make up a concentrated synthetic catnip formula, that is 1,000 times as strong, as regular catnip. We have little doors on Bingo's belly that release the catnip concentrate.

Dr. O'Hara: How do you apply it to attacking lions?

Craig: Watch this. Bingo will run toward the lions then jump over them releasing the catnip on them.

Dr. O'Hara: Lions can jump too you know.

Craig: Remember Bingo is a super bongo and can jump 60 feet.

Dr. Mugadi: Look, it's working. They don't care about the bongo anymore. Good show Craig!
Dr. O'Hara: Whew! How long do we have with these lions in a trance?
Craig: At least an hour.
Craig: Well guys we passed test #4 with the super catnip.
Craig: Well, we did try it out on the zoo lions with the same results.
Dr. O'Hara: Okay, we better take off before they come to their senses.

Dr. Mugadi: Gentlemen, good work today. We should be in Okapi tomorrow.
Dr. Mugadi: Chobe, how's our crew doing?
Chobe: They're fine boss. They are as excited as you guys in saving the bongo herd.
Craig: Looks like the bongo settled down near a river just east of you guys. We need to get some sleep too.
Dr. O'Hara: Okay Craig. Good night.

Craig: Sean. Sean. Oh Sean, wake up.
Craig: Sean, wake up. We have a problem.
Craig: Look at your communicator!
Dr. O'Hara: Craig? What?

Dr. O'Hara: What happened?
Dr. O'Hara: Hippos are very aggressive and territorial. They will come out of the water at night when it's cooler and attack anything around the riverbed. How is the rest of the herd?
Dr. O'Hara: You've got to bring him to us. If we approach the herd, they will stampede.
Dr. O'Hara: Meru, Chobe, wake up.

Craig: Well, that hippo came over, picked up our bongo by the mouth, shook it like a ragdoll, then spit it out!
Craig: They're quiet, laying around, some sleeping. Wait. Sean, something is wrong with Bingo. He's limping on his left rear leg. The hippo must have damaged his leg.
Craig: Stand by.

Craig: I guess a laceration is the same as a rip through the mechanical leg.

Craig: Can you see what's broken? Hold your communicator over the rip or rather the wound.

Craig: The damage looks straight-forward. I'll walk you guys through it. That torn wire needs replacing. If Chobe can take a wire off one of your trucks, like the wire to the horn. Uh, and that bent rod bolts out.

Craig: That rod must be straightened to cure the limp, and that wire supplies power to the lower leg motor.

Dr. O'Hara: Craig, here he comes. Wow, he looks so real. Boy, that's a bad limp. I see a few sparks coming from a laceration.

Dr. O'Hara: Craig, I call it like I see it.

Dr. O'Hara: We're used to working on biological not mechanical animals.

Chobe: Here is the wire Boss.

Dr. Mugadi: Looks like a piston rod is bent and a wire is torn out.

Craig: See, if you guys can do bone surgery on an animal, then you can certainly fix this mechanical leg. We need to hide the gash now.
Craig: Time to test it guys so stand back.
Craig: Great job guys, but don't quit your present jobs yet.

Dr. O'Hara: I know. We will shave some hair off its back, take some medical glue from our medical pack, and glue the hair into the laceration to hide it.
Dr. Mugadi: Sounds good.
Dr. Mugadi: That was fun, and no anesthesia to worry about.
Dr. Mugadi: Put him back to work.
Dr. O'Hara: perfect!

Dr. Mugadi: Well, we are only 10 kilometers away from Okapi. They should be there over the next 1 to 2 hours. Looks like it worked Sean. I'll call Dr. Ruvubi.

Dr. O'Hara: Aren't we going to follow them in the Pegasus all the way on?

Dr. Mugadi: We can't. The terrain from here on is very rough. Our vehicles won't make it.

Dr. O'Hara: Even with the pop-out tires?

Dr. Mugadi: Even with the pop-out tires! I know you want to push that button again. We can follow by foot and call a chopper if needed.

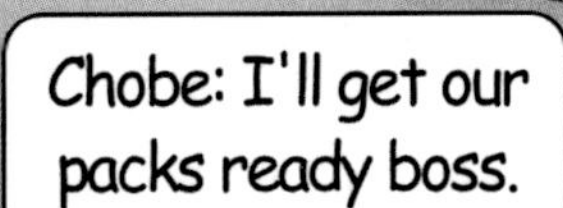
Chobe: I'll get our packs ready boss.

Dr. O'Hara: Meru. Thank you for inviting me to Africa to be part of this team helping the bongo.
Dr. Mugadi: Thank you for coming here. We have to continue to be "the voice for these animals".
Dr. Mugadi: Dr. Ruvubi and his team will be waiting at the Okapi entrance to get a head count.
Chobe: Did you hear that Boss?
Dr. O'Hara: That's gunfire! Who is it?
Dr. Mugadi: Hear what?
Dr. Mugadi: Poachers! It's poachers.

Craig: Sean, I hear you! We've been expecting this. It's time for the poacher-buster-secret weapon!
Craig: Watch this!
Dr. O'Hara: Craig. Help!
Dr. O'Hara: What's the poacher-buster-secret weapon?
Dr. Mugadi: Wow, those bullets are bouncing off Bingo like tse-tse flies!

Craig: The horns are dart riffles with darts made just for poachers.
Craig: We need a little bit of liquid to mix the anesthetic, so we used formic acid. You know, the chemical in bee stings!
Dr. O'Hara: You guys thought of everything. Question. How are those darts made just for poachers?
Dr. Mugadi: That explains the loud, ouch!
Craig: Well, we passed test #5. The poacher darts worked.
Craig: Sorry guys.
Craig: How many bongo did you lose?
Dr. Mugadi: We lost two.

Dr. Mugadi: Over there! The Poachers are all knocked out.
Dr. Mugadi: Go ahead Doc.
Dr. Mugadi: Whew! 10-4.
Dr. Mugadi: 10-4. The poachers are not going anywhere soon.
Dr. Ruvubi: Doc to Meru.
Dr. Ruvubi: My men drove all the bongo into Okapi National Park. The herd is safe, and we will continue to monitor them.
Dr. Ruvubi: I'm headed your way with the police.

Craig: Hey Sean. Bingo has one last feature I have been waiting to show you.
Craig: To celebrate this occasion, the robot has a door that will open on its left side presenting a gift for you guys.
Craig: There was no room for champagne glasses so paper cups will have to do.
Craig: OK we passed the last test. The champagne presentation. Good job guys.

Dr. Mugadi: Wow! A bottle of champagne! A chilled one at that.
Dr. Mugadi: Cheers to saving the bongo!
Dr. Ruvubi: Sean, congratulations and thank you very much.
Dr. Ruvubi: Yes, to saving the bongo!
Dr. O'Hara: Well Craig. What is it?
Dr. O'Hara: Let's have a toast. To saving the bongo!

Guys: Hooray!

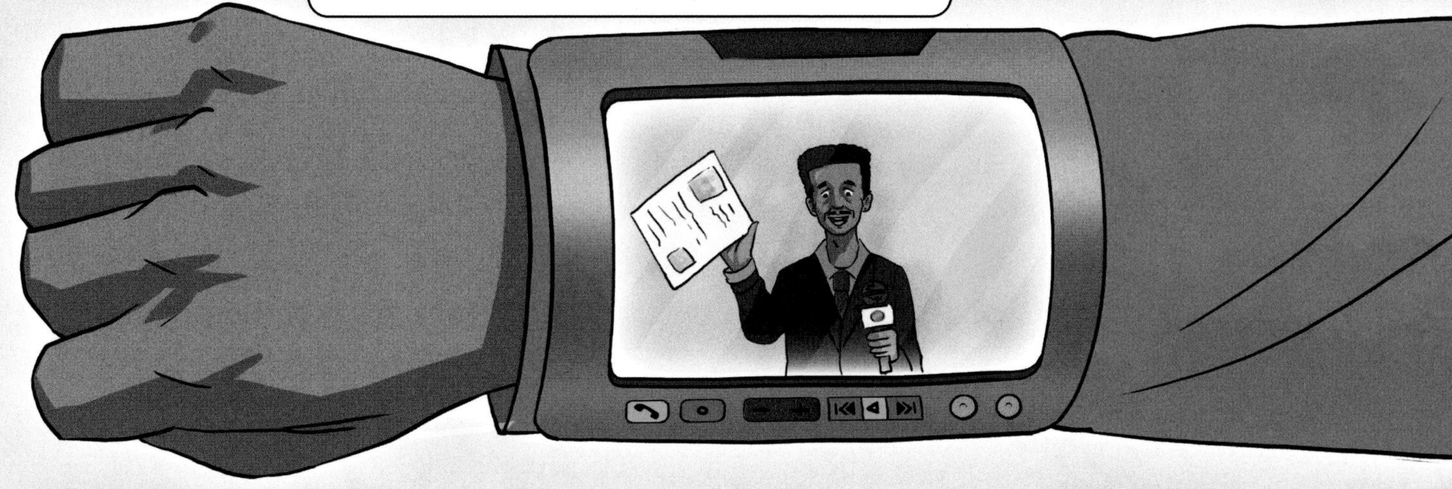
Craig: Craig to Sean, come in.
Craig: I have some bad news back home. It's in your state of Oregon. You know that military toxic depot in Pendleton. Well, a small earthquake this morning damaged some containers causing them to rupture, leaking toxins into a nearby stream.
Craig: No! That stream also feeds into the Columbia River! This is headed to becoming the worst toxic spill in our country.

Dr. Mugadi: Let me guess, the government decided to store these extremely toxic chemicals near this important river?
Dr. O'Hara: Go ahead Craig. What's all the excitement about.
Dr. O'Hara: Yes, I remember about that military storage. During the "cold war", toxic chemicals for chemical warfare were stored there. Craig, can they contain it?
Dr. O'Hara: You see Meru, the Columbia River is this large river dividing Oregon and Washington. There are millions of people, wildlife, and fish living along the river.

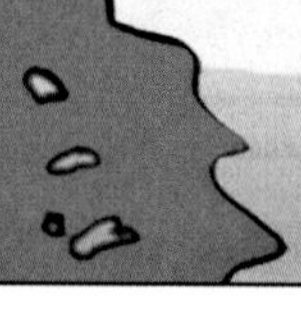

Craig: Sean, I know you wanted to sightsee Africa afterwards, but this bulletin is asking for help from biologists, medical doctors, volunteers, and veterinarians.
Craig: Sean, my students and I are ready to help.

Dr. O'Hara: Okay, but what can I do?
Dr. O'Hara: Okay Craig, will head home ASAP.
Dr. Mugadi: Sean, I've seen you in action and you're the best choice to lead a team, to help with that chemical disaster. We are here to help. We've got to at least try.
Dr. O'Hara: Here's another toast. "I'm the luckiest guy in the world to have friends like you two"
Dr. Ruvubi: Come on guys. Back to work.

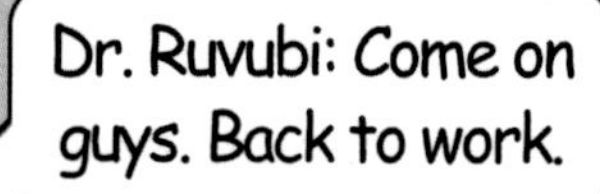

The Adventures of Dr. O'Hara return in the next book, "Poison River".

Bongo (Tragelaphus eurycerus)

Bongo are the largest forest antelope with average weights of about 450 pounds to 800 pounds (205 kgs to 364 kgs). Bongo are browsers and can be found in the Central African countries of Kenya, Uganda, Cameroon, Congo, and Zaine.

Dr. Ruvubi: The Chinook CH-47 is manufactured by Boeing.

Craig: The Hercules C-130 is manufactured by Lockeed-Martin

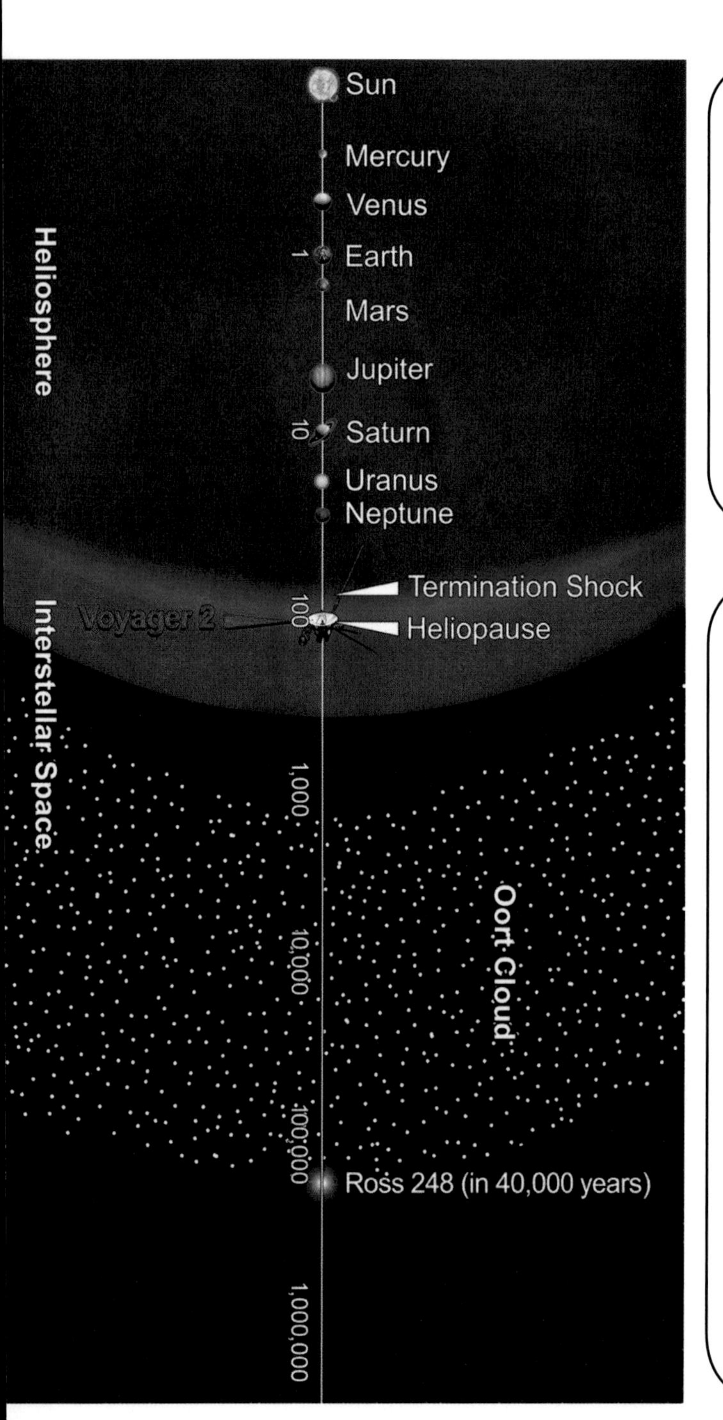

Dr. O'Hara: Voyagers 1 and II are interplanetary vessels built by JPL and were launched in 1977. Their primary mission was to explore Jupiter and Saturn. They continue to fly, are way past Pluto, and in the region called interstellar space (the region between stars). As of 12/11/23, Voyager is over 15 billion miles from earth travelling at 38,026.77 mph, according to the JPL website. They both carry a record, stylus, and instructions on how to operate it. The records have a map of earth's location and messages from, UN secretary Waldheim, and US President Jimmy Carter. It starts with saying hello in 55 languages. There are also many pictures and sounds from earth. Instead of a bottle with a message thrown into the ocean, it is thrown into space. NASA expects contact to be lost in 2025.

Modesto: I remember a great field trip, when I was finishing school, at Glendale Community College, One of my Chemistry teachers took us to, near JPL, in Pasadena for a guided field trip. The tour was amazing and at the end of the tour, we saw a replica of Voyager. The tour guide told us that the Voyager replica was borrowed for an upcoming movie, Star Trek: The Motion Picture. When I saw the movie, I was glad the guide did not spoil the plot, because you are left throughout the movie, wondering who this "Veger" was? Technology is advancing so fast. I am still amazed that the period between Kitty Hawk and the first Lunar Module was only 66 years! Schools, grants, scholarships, social media and societies should promote and invest in more science fields that help care for us, the animals, the environment, and this giant aquarium called planet earth.

About the Author

I have been very fortunate to have worked, as a veterinarian, treating dogs, cats, shelter animals, zoo animals and wildlife. I was influenced by TV animal and nature shows and admired their heroes: James Harriet, Marlin Perkins, Jim Fowler, Jane Goodall, Jacques Cousteau, and Sir David Attenborough. It's true, "What's bad for the beehive is bad for the bees".

Modesto

Printed in the United States
by Baker & Taylor Publisher Services